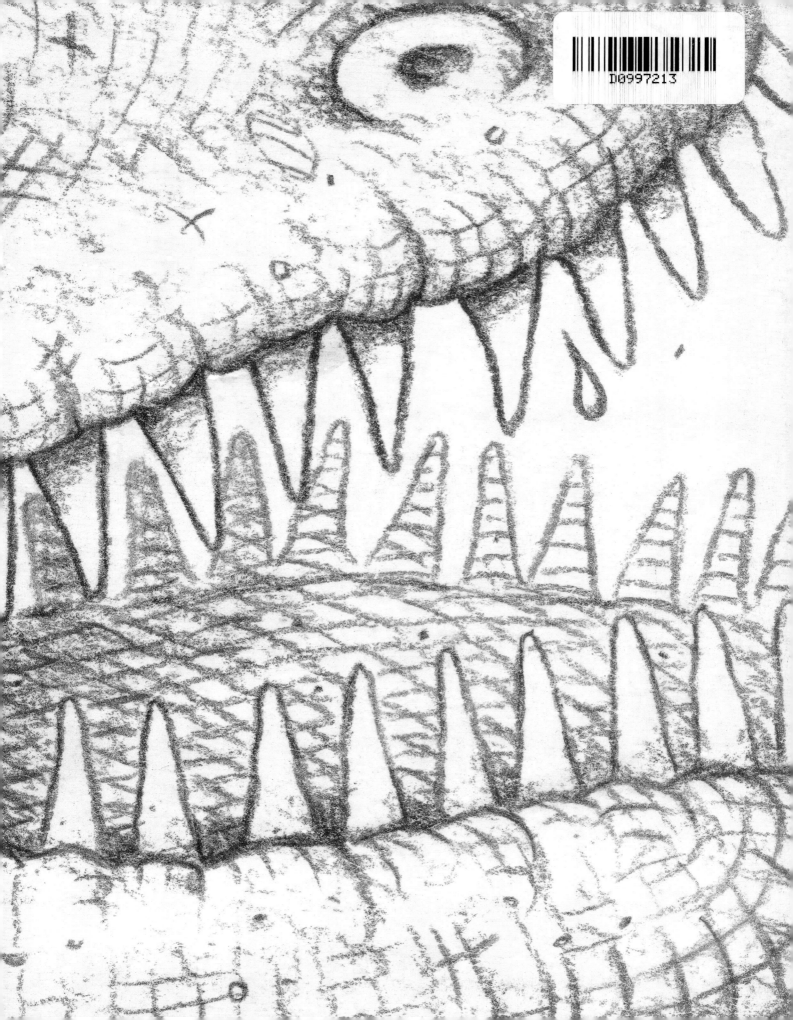

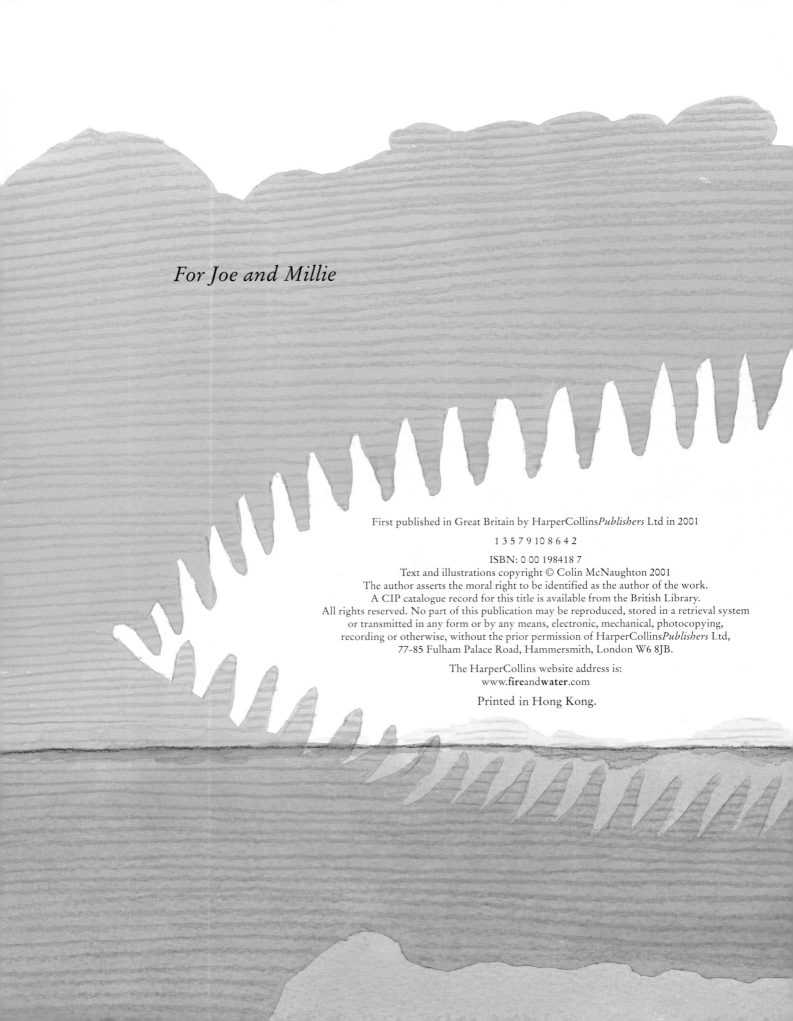

For Joe and Millie

First published in Great Britain by HarperCollins*Publishers* Ltd in 2001

1 3 5 7 9 10 8 6 4 2

ISBN: 0 00 198418 7

Text and illustrations copyright © Colin McNaughton 2001

The HarperCollins website address is:
www.**fire**and**water**.com

Printed in Hong Kong.

Colin McNaughton

Collins

An imprint of HarperCollins*Publishers*

Good news!
You've
got the
day off.
Hooray!

Bad news!
To go
to the
dentist.
Boo!

Go!

Good news!
You don't meet *those* boys on the way.
Hooray!

Bad news!
You meet *those* girls.
Boo!

Good news!
One of your
teachers comes by.
Hooray!

Bad news!
The one who doesn't like you.
Boo!

Bad news!
By aliens.
Boo!

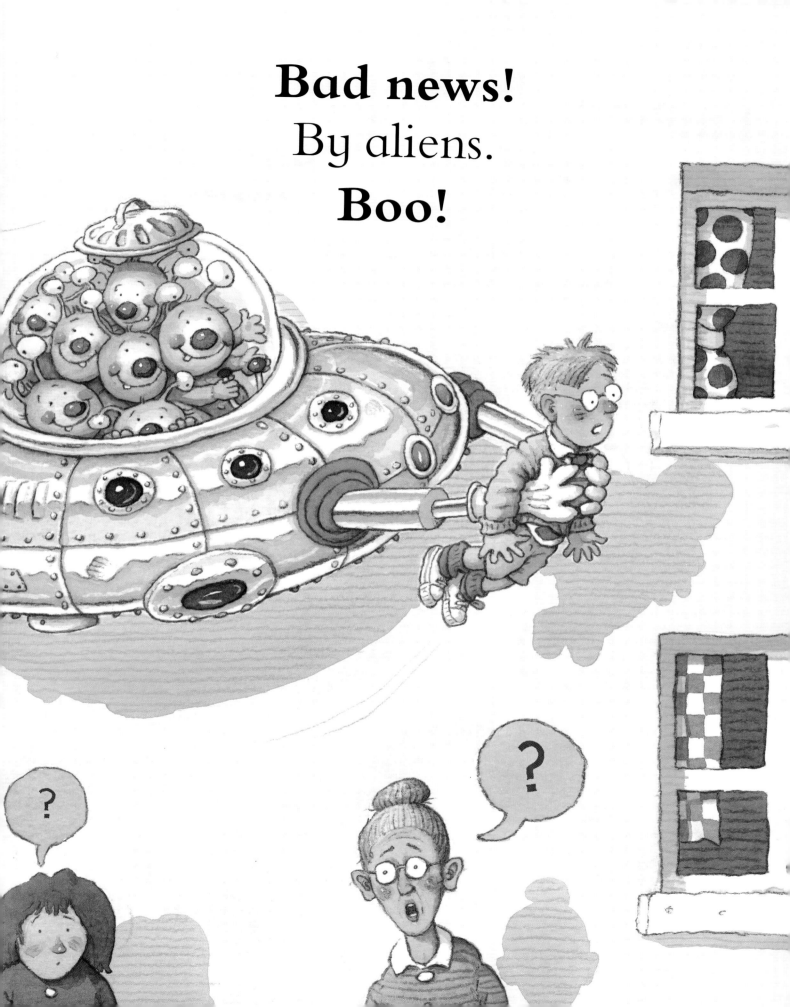

Good news!
They're friendly.
Hooray!

Bad news!
They smell like babies' nappies.
Poo!

Good news!
They let you go.
Hooray!

Bad news!
Without a parachute.
Boo!

Good news!
You land on something soft.
Hooray!

Bad news!
A big hairy monster.
Boo!

Good news!
Something chases him off.
Hooray!

Bad news!
A herd of elephants.
Boo!

Good news!
They get chased off.
Hooray!

Bad news!
By a Tyrannosaurus Rex.
Boo!

Good news!
You're saved just in time.
Hooray!

Bad news!
By a witch.
Boo!

Good news!
You jump from the
witch's broomstick.
Hooray!

Bad news!
You land on your
dentist's head.
Boo!

Good news!
He's not hurt.
Hooray!

Bad news!
You're just in time for
your dental appointment.
Boo!

Good news!
It doesn't hurt a bit.
Hooray!

Bad news!
Your dentist is
Count Dracula.
Boo!

Good news!
You escape and
reach home safely.
Hooray!

Bad news!
There *is* no more
bad news.
Hooray!

Absolutely
fangtastic!

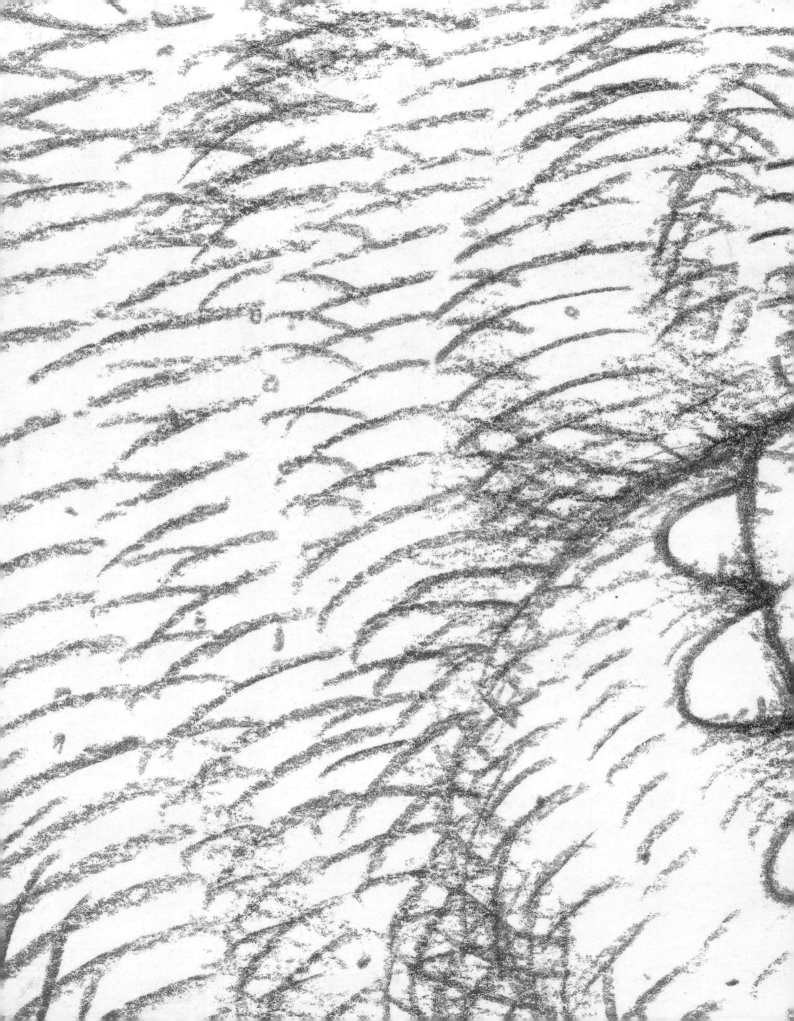